Samuel French Acting Edition

Friend Art

by Sofia Alvarez

SAMUELFRENCH.COM SAMUELFRENCH.CO.UK

FOR PRODUCTION ENQUIRIES

UNITED STATES AND CANADA
Info@SamuelFrench.com
1-866-598-8449

UNITED KINGDOM AND EUROPE
Plays@SamuelFrench.co.uk
020-7255-4302

Each title is subject to availability from Samuel French, depending upon
country of performance. Please be aware that FRIEND ART may not be
licensed by Samuel French in your territory. Professional and amateur
producers should contact the nearest Samuel French office or licensing
partner to verify availability.

MUSIC USE NOTE

Licensees are solely responsible for obtaining formal written permission from copyright owners to use copyrighted music in the performance of this play and are strongly cautioned to do so. If no such permission is obtained by the licensee, then the licensee must use only original music that the licensee owns and controls. Licensees are solely responsible and liable for all music clearances and shall indemnify the copyright owners of the play(s) and their licensing agent, Samuel French, against any costs, expenses, losses and liabilities arising from the use of music by licensees. Please contact the appropriate music licensing authority in your territory for the rights to any incidental music.

IMPORTANT BILLING AND CREDIT REQUIREMENTS

If you have obtained performance rights to this title, please refer to your licensing agreement for important billing and credit requirements.

Friend Art was first produced by Second Stage Theatre in New York City in May of 2016. The performance was directed by Portia Krieger, with sets by Daniel Zimmerman, costumes by Ásta Bennie Hostetter, lighting design by Mike Inwood, and original music and sound design by Palmer Hefferan. The Production Stage Manager was Kathryn "China" Hayzer and the Stage Manager was Shanna Allison. The cast was as follows:

MOLLY.. Zoe Chao

KEVIN .... Aaron Costa Ganis

NATE ....Constantine Maroulis

LIL... Anabelle LeMieux

CHARACTERS

MOLLY – (thirty-ish) The office manager of a law firm in Manhattan. Any ethnicity.

KEVIN – (thirty-ish) Works in corporate art, Molly's fiancé. Any ethnicity.

NATE – (thirty-five-ish) A rock star in the days of Matchbox Twenty and Lit. Kevin's childhood friend. Any ethnicity.

LIL – (twenty-four) A performance artist and former assistant at Molly's office, Nate's ex-girlfriend. Any ethnicity.

SETTING

NYC

TIME

2010s

Scenes 1 & 2: A night in April

Scenes 3-7: A night in May

Scenes 8 & 9: The next weekend

Scene 10: A couple of weeks later

Scenes 11-13: A night in June

Scene 14: The next day

Scene 15: An afternoon in October

AUTHOR'S NOTES

On casting: This play is about artists in New York City, so while none of the actors are listed as specific races or ethnicities, they should be as diverse a group as the city in which they live. I've always thought of Nate as white – mainly because the references for his band are Matchbox Twenty and Lit – but he by no means has to be.

On the performance art: Lil takes her art very seriously, so the actor (and production) should as well. While the play is a comedy, it does not work if the performance art is played as a joke.

1. A Black Box Theater

(Blackout.)

(Spotlight on **LIL**'s *face. The rest of her body is in darkness – we can only see her floating head.)*

LIL. I'm really good at scaring myself. Left alone in the dark, within minutes I'll have myself convinced something is about to grab my toe.

I had a recurring nightmare as a child that I'd look out my bedroom window and a large snake would be staring at me. We'd make eye contact after which I could not pretend he wasn't there. He knows I've seen him and so now he can get me, I thought. Maybe if I play dead he'll go away. Lie still, pull the covers over your head and try to shake the feeling something bad is coming.

(Beat.)

LIL. And something bad is coming.

(A gong sounds.)

(A cantaloupe drops from the ceiling.)

(A gong sounds again.)

(The cantaloupe starts to spin.)

(A gong sounds for a third time.)

*(***LIL*** disappears.)*

(Blackout.)

(Lights up on **MOLLY** *and* **KEVIN** *standing around after the performance.)*

KEVIN. Something bad was coming alright.

MOLLY. Stop it.

KEVIN. I mean, talk about a warning.

MOLLY. It was good.

KEVIN. Babe. It was not good.

MOLLY. There were good parts.

KEVIN. There were no good parts. Guess Nate got out just in time.

MOLLY. What do you mean?

KEVIN. Like they broke up just in time for him not to have to see it. If I had to watch you in something like that –

MOLLY. I never did performance art. And my plays were not this bad.

KEVIN. No, but they wouldn't have to be that good to be better than this.

MOLLY. Alright buddy, get your kicks out now. Because once she comes out, you have to be nice. We're here supporting our friend.

KEVIN. I'm just glad we don't have to go to many more of these.

MOLLY. What do you mean?

KEVIN. No performance art in Virginia.

MOLLY. So you think.

KEVIN. Babe. If we're going to shit like this after we move, kill me.

MOLLY. Oh, shh, shh, you have to be nice now. Here she comes...

       (**LIL** *walks up.*)

LIL. Hi you guys!

       (*She gives them both hugs.*)

MOLLY. Oh my god. Lil. So good!

LIL. Thank you so much for coming.

MOLLY. Of course. This was really exciting.

LIL. You really think so?

MOLLY. Really, I was like – I was seriously blown away. That thing you did with that revolving cantaloupe and...the bees. I just found it – well I found it really powerful.

LIL. Yeah, this was a big one. Lots of moving pieces.

MOLLY. Kevin?

KEVIN. Yep.

MOLLY. What did you think?

KEVIN. Yeah, great stuff Lil.

LIL. Did Nate come with you guys?

KEVIN. Why would Nate come?

MOLLY. Kevin.

KEVIN. What? They broke up.

LIL. We're still friends.

KEVIN. Sorry, none of my business.

LIL. Well – anyway. I'm glad you guys were able to make it.

MOLLY. So, is there a next step?

LIL. Well, I don't know. We have a couple more shows this weekend. I'm hoping someone comes to review it because then I could maybe do another week.

KEVIN. But it would have to be a good review.

LIL. Yeah.

KEVIN. Hm.

MOLLY. I'm crossing my fingers they come.

LIL. Thanks.

MOLLY. Drinks? Are we getting drinks?

LIL. You know, I should probably rest for tomorrow.

KEVIN. So no drinks. Great. Let's go babe.

MOLLY. Congratulations again!

(**NATE** *walks up.*)

NATE. Hey turds.

LIL. Hey! You're here!

NATE. 'Course. I wouldn't miss this. Good work kid. Get in here.

(*He goes to hug* **LIL** *then gives her a noogie instead.*)

That's my girl. Arty shit. I love it. Where we drinking?

MOLLY. We were gonna –

NATE. No way – I'm buying. What's around here? That bar. The one with the shiny tables. Let's go.

MOLLY. Is that okay, Lil? Didn't you want to rest?

LIL. Well you know, one drink or whatever can't hurt.

NATE. Great. We out.

>(**NATE** *and* **LIL** *walk ahead of* **MOLLY** *and* **KEVIN.**)

MOLLY. Is this okay?

KEVIN. Sure, sure. The place with the shiny tables. What could be better?

2. The Place With The Shiny Tables

(**NATE**, **KEVIN**, and **MOLLY** *sit at a table with drinks.* **LIL** *is in the bathroom.*)

KEVIN. It really comes down to loyalty, right? I mean look at me and Molly. We love each other and so – we don't cheat. It's simple.

NATE. Yeah except it's not always that simple.

KEVIN. How so?

NATE. Well, I loved Lil, I still may love Lil, but I cheated on her. Not simple.

KEVIN. But see, to me, that means you don't love her.

NATE. Love can mean a lot of different things.

KEVIN. Yeah and one of them is that you shouldn't cheat on your partner. Unless – your partner's not that important to you. Which maybe, she's not.

NATE. Disagree.

KEVIN. Why are you fighting me so hard on this when you know I'm right?

NATE. You're not right on this one, man. This isn't like Penelope Vasquez.

MOLLY. Who's Penelope Vasquez?

NATE. She was Kevin's girlfriend freshman year of high school.

KEVIN. Girlfriend is an overstatement.

MOLLY. You dated someone I don't know about?

KEVIN. No. We went to a dance together or something. I don't know.

NATE. He knows. Anyway. Kevin was obsessed with her and he thought they were dating and they definitely weren't and she hooked up with someone else and he freaked out.

KEVIN. This is irrelevant.

MOLLY. No. This is amazing. Babe, I never get to hear a story about you that I don't already know. Nate, what else?

NATE. That's basically it but that's why Kev's so freaked out about even the idea of infidelity. It all goes back to Penelope Vasquez and his tiny, fourteen-year-old, broken heart.

MOLLY. Babe, is that true? That's adorable.

KEVIN. *(To* **MOLLY.***)* It's an exaggeration based in a mild truth.

(To **NATE.***)* But it has nothing to do with you and Lil.

NATE. *(To* **MOLLY.***)* Also, I might have been the guy she hooked up with.

MOLLY. Damn, Penelope. Get it girl.

KEVIN. This is ridiculous, that story has nothing to do with anything we were talking about. Nate just doesn't want to admit that he cheated on Lil because she's not that important to him.

LIL. Excuse me, Kevin?

KEVIN. Aw, shit.

> *(***LIL** *hands* **NATE** *his wallet and sits back down at the table.)*

NATE. Kevin thinks the fact that I cheated on you means I don't love you.

LIL. Fuck you, Kevin.

KEVIN. Oh my god. Dude, seriously? Lil – I'm sorry. I shouldn't have said anything. Let's change the subject.

LIL. No, by all means – go ahead. I would rather you talk about me in front of me than behind my back.

KEVIN. I was being an asshole and I'm sorry. You guys are doing whatever you're doing and that's great. Can we drop it?

MOLLY. Why would you rather him talk about it in front of you?

KEVIN. Molly. Please. Don't get involved.

MOLLY. I'm curious. I don't understand why she wants to talk about it at all. I mean if you ever cheated on me –

LIL. Well – we're different Molly. If Kevin cheated on you, you would probably never speak to him again, in fact none of us would see each other or be friends – all on account of an act that you would say is private when in fact by not talking about it, it would become very public. I'm not that well – I don't want to say selfish, but, part of me thinks selfish is a good word for it. Yes, Nate cheated on me. Yes, I was sad, we broke up – things are now, complicated. But, we're all still out together, having a drink and talking about it and you know what? That makes it hurt less. So Kevin giving his opinion that this one act means Nate doesn't love me – well I absolutely want to hear it.

MOLLY. I don't get it.

KEVIN. Who needs another drink?

NATE. Everybody. I'll help you.

KEVIN. Babe, you want another Manhattan?

MOLLY. No, no. Just a beer. Will you get me a Peroni?

KEVIN. K. Lil?

LIL. Whatever you guys are getting.

                    (The men walk away.)

MOLLY. You don't really believe all of that do you? You're just trying to be laid-back about it in front of Nate?

LIL. I absolutely believe it.

                    (Small beat.)

   I'm also a little high.

MOLLY. What?

LIL. Nate and I have been doing bumps in the bathroom.

MOLLY. Are you serious?

LIL. Just little ones.

MOLLY. Oh my god. Lil. I can't believe you're back with Nate.

LIL. We're not together-together.

MOLLY. So what are you?

LIL. I guess we're dating.

MOLLY. Dating? You were living together.

LIL. Never officially. I always had my apartment.

MOLLY. Your apartment is your childhood bedroom at your parents' house.

LIL. You know, I really don't understand why you're being so mean to me on my night.

MOLLY. Your night?

LIL. Yes, this is the night of my show and we are supposed to be celebrating, but instead you just keep picking at me and haven't even told me what you thought.

MOLLY. I did tell you.

LIL. You told me you liked the cantaloupe and the bees.

MOLLY. I did!

LIL. But that was just one little part, what about the rest of it?

MOLLY. I thought it was good.

LIL. That means you hated it.

MOLLY. It does not.

LIL. In case you've forgotten, we used to do this together.

MOLLY. Do what?

LIL. Find one thing you liked, single it out, smile and say congratulations. I know that means you hated it.

MOLLY. It doesn't! I always tell you when I like things.

LIL. But I'm not just looking for generic praise. I want to know *why* you liked the things you liked.

MOLLY. So you're looking for specific praise?

LIL. Oh my god would you stop attacking me?

MOLLY. I'm not attacking you. I feel like you're attacking me. I feel I am a very supportive friend to you. I don't know what else I can do to show you that –

LIL. You can tell me the truth. I can handle it.

MOLLY. Okay.

LIL. Okay.

MOLLY. Okay. If I'm being totally honest…I didn't really get it. It didn't make a lot of sense to me.
    But you know maybe I'm not smart enough or something. Maybe it went over my head.

LIL. Oh my god. Do not patronize me, Molly.

MOLLY. No, Lil. I'm not. I did like some of it. And you know, it's really ambitious to do, like, everything yourself and you are clearly very talented. And honestly I really envy that you were able to quit the firm and become a full-time artist. I think that's really brave. And that's not BS, that's true. But, I just didn't really like the...show.

LIL. Okay.

MOLLY. Okay what?

LIL. Okay thank you for your honesty.

MOLLY. Now you're mad at me.

LIL. I'm not.

MOLLY. You are, you're using your polite voice. You asked me to tell you what I thought!

LIL. I know and you did so thanks. Thanks for coming.

MOLLY. I can't win.

LIL. I mean I guess if I was still working some shitty office job my views would be colored by the corporate world too.

MOLLY. Hey. That's not fair.

(The men return with the drinks.)

KEVIN. They were out of Peroni so I got you a Newcastle.

MOLLY. Why would you get me a Newcastle? That's like an entirely different kind of beer.

KEVIN. Sorry, babe. They were out.

MOLLY. Did they have Stella or something comparable?

KEVIN. I don't know we were all getting Newcastles so I got you one.

LIL. Hey Nate, do you wanna get out of here?

NATE. No, I just bought all these drinks.

LIL. I'm tired.

MOLLY. Oh my god. You're not tired.

LIL. I'm tired and I want to leave and if you want to come with me –

MOLLY. You can't be tired you're on coke.

KEVIN. You told her?!

MOLLY. You're on coke too??

KEVIN. I –

MOLLY. So everyone is on coke but me??

NATE. Yeah because I thought you didn't do drugs.

MOLLY. That is not the point.

LIL. Nate, can we just get out of here, please?

NATE. I don't want to leave yet.

LIL. I just kinda wanna go home.

MOLLY. You're not gonna go home you're going to go to another bar and talk shit about me.

NATE. Can't we just talk shit about you here? It's raining.

LIL. You guys do whatever you want. I'm leaving. Nate, if you wanted to come with me. That would be cool. If not, well, not.

(*LIL exits.*)

NATE. Man. You'd think when you weren't dating someone anymore you wouldn't have to put up with all their bullshit.

(*He stands up and slams his drink.*)

Night fellas.

(*NATE exits. MOLLY looks at KEVIN.*)

MOLLY. And I cannot believe you did coke.

3. An Art Gallery

(**MOLLY** *stands by a cheese platter. She's self-consciously-but-hungrily eating cubes of cheese and crackers.* **NATE** *walks up to her from behind, startling her.*)

NATE. Hungry?

MOLLY. Hi? Yeah, I'm starving. I came straight from work. What are you doing here?

NATE. I'm friends with one of the artists. What are you doing here?

MOLLY. My boss is married to one of them. She was worried no one would be here for her work specifically. Group show, you know?

NATE. Yep.

MOLLY. I don't really know anyone here.

NATE. Me neither.

MOLLY. What about your friend?

NATE. He's more of an acquaintance really.

MOLLY. Oh, I get it.

NATE. What?

MOLLY. You got paid.

(**NATE** *shrugs.*)

Your job is so weird.

NATE. It's not a job really, it's just something I do once in a while to get out of the house.

MOLLY. It's like rent-a-used-to-be-somewhat-famous-friend.

NATE. But you get me for free.

MOLLY. I'm touched.

(**MOLLY** *takes another piece of cheese.*)

NATE. How's the cheese?

MOLLY. Fine. Cheesy. How's Lil?

NATE. Haven't talked to her in awhile.

MOLLY. Oh. So you guys aren't –

NATE. No.

MOLLY. Oh, sorry.

NATE. It's cool. She's working on some new thing and she said I was distracting her or she was "distracted" by not knowing what was going on with us.

MOLLY. That is so her.

NATE. Did you guys ever resolve your little thing?

MOLLY. What thing?

NATE. You know – whatever it was? That bullshit from the bar awhile ago. I thought Lil overreacted.

MOLLY. Oh that was nothing – I've just been really busy.

NATE. Got it.

MOLLY. And she is too, apparently.

NATE. Yeah.

>   *(Small beat.)*

>   How's work?

MOLLY. Good.

NATE. Your boss still making you do all kinds of crazy shit that has nothing to do with your job?

MOLLY. Yeah, that's, you know, why I'm here.

NATE. Oh right, you said. That sucks. You should quit.

MOLLY. I don't mind actually. Sometimes it's fun.

NATE. Oh yeah?

MOLLY. Yeah, like he was hiding this affair a little while ago and needed my help with it. And I mean, I know most people might think that's really despicable and wouldn't want to take part in it but I actually thought it was pretty interesting to see how someone would go about lying that elaborately – so I didn't mind, like, booking the hotel rooms and helping hide it from his wife – I got overtime.

NATE. Cool?

MOLLY. Sorry. I shouldn't have told you that. Especially here, at her opening. I don't want you to think that I'm

like okay with people having affairs – I'm totally not.
But this was for work.

NATE. Don't worry. I know you're principled.

MOLLY. Right.

> *(Small beat.)*

NATE. How's Kev?

MOLLY. He's good.

NATE. Things good with you guys?

MOLLY. Yep.

NATE. You're picking out cakes and stuff?

MOLLY. Uh-huh.

NATE. Nice. Love that guy.

MOLLY. Me too, obviously.

NATE. I should call him, tell him to feed you better.

MOLLY. Excuse me?

> *(**NATE** strokes her arm with his finger.)*

NATE. Bird arms. Too skinny.

> *(**MOLLY** pulls her arm away.)*

MOLLY. Okay.

NATE. You look good, Mol.

MOLLY. Thanks.

NATE. You seem happy.

MOLLY. I am happy.

NATE. Good. I'm glad to hear it.

MOLLY. Uh-huh.

NATE. Don't do that. Don't dismiss it. It's true. I really care
about you. You and Kev – the dream, man.

MOLLY. We appreciate your support.

NATE. Why are you going hard on me?

MOLLY. I'm not.

NATE. *(Taunting.)* Molly...

MOLLY. What?

NATE. Tell me what's up.

MOLLY. Well.

NATE. Yeah.

MOLLY. I'm just kind of uncomfortable because I feel like you're hitting on me.

NATE. You do?

MOLLY. Aren't you?

NATE. No.

MOLLY. Oh.

> *(Small beat.)*

Then I'm embarrassed.

> *(She looks around the room.)*

NATE. You can be really uptight sometimes.

MOLLY. I'm just really hungry. I want to get out of here.

NATE. Do you see your boss around?

MOLLY. No.

NATE. So leave.

MOLLY. I would feel bad.

NATE. That's your problem, always feeling bad. Always helping people cheat then feeling bad about it.

MOLLY. What? No, I –

NATE. Relax. I'm teasing. But if you don't want to be here, you should leave.

MOLLY. Okay.

NATE. Okay what?

MOLLY. I guess I'm leaving then.

> *(**MOLLY** grabs her things and quickly exits, leaving **NATE** standing awkwardly alone.)*

NATE. The fuck?

4. A Black Box Theater (Another One)

*(Spotlight up on **LIL**.)*

(One of her hands is behind her back.)

LIL. Did you ever imagine an animal was in bed with you?
A fly? A spider? A mouse? A rat? A snake?

*(**LIL** is still.)*

Sssssssssss. What's that? Sssssssssss.

*(**LIL** reveals her hidden hand, and we see that
she is wearing a childlike snake puppet that
goes all the way up her arm.)*

Look at that. There's a snake in my bed and I didn't
even notice. Am I really not afraid of him? Or is it that
he's tricked me into thinking he's my friend?

(The snake moves.)

Sssssssssss. We make eye contact and I pause. I know
those eyes. Those are my lover's eyes. Is my lover the
snake? He tells me I shouldn't be so scared, if I'm lying
with the one I love.

I'm not scared, I think, but I am guarded. Worse maybe.
The snake's told me before that he's in my head and
maybe I should believe him, because he does always
seem to be there.

He's in my head as a way to get into my body.

*(**LIL** sinks onto the floor and begins to roll
around with the snake.)*

This is what I wanted, I think. This is what I've been
wanting. Me and the snake, together. I must have his
attention now. He can't be ignoring me if he found his
way to my bed.

*(**LIL** moves the snake puppet down toward her
vagina, and we get the impression she might
be about to masturbate onstage.)*

He hisses in my ear.

(Thank goodness, the puppet is back by her head.)

LIL. "I know you," he says. "I know you better than you know yourself."

(She stops.)

Wait. It doesn't feel right anymore. Why is he paying attention to me now? What's different about me now other than my naked body? No, it can't be that. If I went to his snake job naked he would hate it. He would hate me. Privacy is the difference, that must be the difference. But he's the one who withholds that from me... He's the one who withholds.

(She pauses.)

He loves me now, I think, but he can still ignore me tomorrow.

(She turns the puppet to the front so that it faces and addresses the audience.)

(As the snake, in whatever voice he would use.) "If I let her give me away, I can never be responsible for losing her."

*(**LIL** looks at the puppet. She makes it go limp in her hand. She looks at the audience and recites a poem.)*

He's soft now and I can rest.
If I let him stay and hold him,
will he love me more or less?
It's going to be so awkward
when we see each other,
Tomorrow,
on the internet.

(She slowly bows her head.)

(We hear a couple of people clap.)

Thank you.

5. The Street

(**KEVIN** *walks up to* **LIL** *after her performance.*)

KEVIN. Great, job. Lil.

LIL. Kevin. Hi.

KEVIN. I thought that was great.

LIL. Thanks. Is Molly with you?

KEVIN. She's working late tonight, but I wanted to check it out.

LIL. That's nice of you. You really didn't have to.

KEVIN. My office is right around the corner so why not, right?

LIL. Well I appreciate it –

KEVIN. Also, we haven't seen you in awhile. Worried about you, kiddo.

LIL. Thanks – I've just been busy with this and you know – stuff.

KEVIN. I know Molly would love to see you.

LIL. I wish she had come.

KEVIN. I'm sure she wanted to – just, you know, work.

LIL. I know, I understand. It's just at these solo shows every audience member counts.

KEVIN. Not exactly killing it, huh?

LIL. You could say that.

KEVIN. Maybe if you made it more of a show. Like, there's this group of female performance artists that market themselves as a band and their shows are always packed.

LIL. Right, um, I'm not trying to be mean – I really appreciate that you came. But it's kind of a low to work really hard on something and then have no one there to see it so I'm not really in the mood for one of my non-artist friends to try and tell me how to be a better artist. But seriously, thanks, it was nice of you to come.

(*She starts to go. He follows her.*)

KEVIN. Hey Lil.

LIL. Yeah?

KEVIN. I'm not a non-artist.

LIL. What?

KEVIN. Okay, I may not be an artist like you are. But I am a curator and I'm trying to help you.

LIL. You're not a curator, Kevin.

KEVIN. Yes I am. I get paid to curate. I'm a curator.

LIL. You decide what to put on office walls.

KEVIN. Corporations have a lot more money to play with than individuals.

LIL. I'm sorry. Your job is really important.

KEVIN. Do you wanna get a drink?

LIL. What? No. Why?

KEVIN. Because you're right. It sucks to work hard on something and have no one there to see it. But I did see it and I thought it was interesting. So let me buy you a drink to celebrate.

        (Small beat.)

LIL. Um, how are things with you and Molly?

KEVIN. Good.

LIL. Wedding planning and stuff is good?

KEVIN. Yeah, why?

LIL. I don't know. Just a question.

KEVIN. You don't trust me.

LIL. I'm just in a really vulnerable place when I come out of a performance and you're catching me totally off guard here. You usually hate my stuff.

KEVIN. No, I don't.

LIL. Yes, you do. And you're a bad liar.

KEVIN. You're right, I am. So if I'm telling you that I was intrigued by this one, and you believe me, it must be the truth.

LIL. Okay, that's fair. But. If *I'm* being totally honest I think it's a little weird that you want to get a drink with me solo. Like, why did you even come here tonight?

KEVIN. Truth?

(She nods.)

Like I said, my office is around the corner. I was taking a walk on my lunch break and I saw you setting up.

(Small beat.)

I was curious.

LIL. You were curious about me?

KEVIN. Your last show was only a few weeks ago and I thought how much more could she possibly have to say?

LIL. I still can't tell if you're making fun of me or not.

KEVIN. Come on. One drink. I'm buying.

6. Molly And Kevin's Apartment

>(**MOLLY** *enters the apartment she shares with* **KEVIN.**)

MOLLY. Kev?

>(*He's not there. She puts her things down. Takes off her jacket.*)

Hm.

>(*She changes into pajamas and goes to the kitchen, looks in the fridge. Nothing. She pours herself a bowl of cereal.*)

>(*A knock at the door.*)

(*Calling out as she goes to answer it.*) Hey babe. Did you forget your keys?

>(**MOLLY** *opens the door, holding her bowl of cereal. It's* **NATE.**)

Nate!

NATE. Are you mad at me?

MOLLY. Why would I be mad at you?

NATE. You stormed out of the opening.

MOLLY. No I didn't. I left. You're sweating. Do you want some water or something?

NATE. Where's Kev?

MOLLY. I dunno. Probably working late.

>(*He looks around.*)

NATE. Man, I feel like I haven't been over here in awhile.

MOLLY. You haven't.

NATE. You guys got new furniture.

MOLLY. Just the chair.

NATE. It's so married couple in here.

MOLLY. Well, we're getting married.

NATE. I know, crazy!

MOLLY. Nate. You're old. Your friends getting married isn't crazy.

NATE. I know! And *that's* what's crazy about it.

MOLLY. Sorry. What are you doing here?

NATE. What do you mean? I wanna hang out.

MOLLY. With me? Just me? Like without Kev?

NATE. Yeah who cares?

MOLLY. Um...okay.

NATE. Why are you being weird?

MOLLY. I'm not.

NATE. You are. You're always so weird around me. Why are you always so weird around me?

MOLLY. I dunno. Maybe it's because whenever we see you I always assume you're like, wishing we were cooler or something.

NATE. What? That's crazy. I don't want you guys to be cool.

MOLLY. Thanks.

NATE. No. I mean, Molly. Obviously you're cool. And Kev is like the coolest guy ever. But I like that you guys are just like, "my friends" and not you know like "cool."

MOLLY. And here I always thought I was a second-tier friend when it turns out I'm actually just a loser friend.

NATE. How could you ever think you were second-tier? Kevin is like my oldest friend!

MOLLY. Okay, sure. Kevin is your oldest friend but I'm just Kevin's girlfriend.

NATE. Molly, come on. You guys have been together forever. You're not just Kevin's girlfriend to me.

MOLLY. I'm not talking about that. I know we have history. But the older you get don't you kind of start to feel like you have history with everyone? I've been awkwardly running into the same people on the street for years but it doesn't mean they're my friends.

NATE. You're comparing me to people you run into on the street? Are you kidding me? That is so offensive. You guys are like my best friends.

MOLLY. Yeah but you say that about everyone. I've heard you
     call the guys who work at that seedy liquor store near
     your loft your best friends.

NATE. Those guys are seriously like, some of my best friends.

MOLLY. Right.

NATE. What?!

MOLLY. Nothing. I'm just not sure what we're supposed to
     talk about.

NATE. God. You're so awkward.

MOLLY. I am not.

NATE. Yes, you are.

MOLLY. Well, sorry I'm not like, as cool as your music
     friends or your liquor store friends.

NATE. Why do you keep saying you're not cool? I think
     you're cool.

MOLLY. I don't know.

NATE. Anyway, I'm not cool either. It's not like I was in
     some band that people respect.

MOLLY. Are you kidding? People loved you. You were so
     good.

          (*Singing, getting into it.*)

     "YOU'RE CLIMBING UP MY THROAAAT.
     I'M DIGGING IN MY HEELS."

NATE. Stop it.

MOLLY. Don't you ever miss it? If I were you, I would miss
     it so much.

NATE. I miss performing. I miss my band. But I also miss
     like being poor. And even hanging out with you guys,
     like, two years ago when you would still at least pretend
     that you were fun.

MOLLY. Thanks.

NATE. I just feel so fucking old, you know? Like I'm nostalgic
     for everything, even things I hated.

MOLLY. Like hanging out with us.

NATE. It's like – it's like I only know how to be happy in my memories.

MOLLY. Why don't you try and feel a little more sorry for yourself?

NATE. I'm serious, Molly! Like, take Lil for example. She wanted to move in with me and I was all, "Nah, I'm good." But then she just started sleeping over every night. And I could've just enjoyed living with this girl who doesn't give a shit that I don't want to do any of the traditional stuff like you guys and yeah she's kinda nuts and never cleans up after herself – but it's okay because I have a cleaning lady so it's not like we'd get in fights about it, though I would've liked her to at least once acknowledge that Lorena was cleaning up after her and the mess wasn't just like disappearing, but that's a tangent because actually we were pretty happy – but I don't know how to deal with that so what did I do? I cheated on her. She moved out and now I miss her.

MOLLY. So what's next Nate? What's next can be exciting.

NATE. Yeah for you guys. You guys are getting married. But Lil and I, we are definitely not getting married.

MOLLY. Do you want to marry Lil?

NATE. No. I don't want to marry anyone. But I also don't want to go home to my empty apartment every night.

MOLLY. Is that why you came over here?

(He gives her a cute and pathetic look.)

Aw. Are you hungry? Do you want something to eat?

NATE. Okay.

MOLLY. Okay yes?

NATE. Yeah.

MOLLY. Cereal okay? There is like nothing in there.

NATE. Do you have bananas?

MOLLY. We do.

NATE. Okay – that'd be great.

(*She pours him a bowl of cereal, cuts bananas into it.*)

NATE. It's so nice over here.

(*She hands him the bowl.*)

MOLLY. You could have an apartment like this.

NATE. No I couldn't. This is an "I live with a girl" apartment.

MOLLY. You could "live with a girl."

NATE. Lil and I lived together and my apartment never looked like this.

MOLLY. You guys were never interested in this kind of life – you were never the couple who wanted to go home at ten.

NATE. Lil was never that girl.

MOLLY. And you were never that guy.

NATE. I want to meet that girl.

MOLLY. You will, if that's what you want.

NATE. But she has to be like – the best version of that girl.

MOLLY. She's out there.

NATE. No, I mean – she has to be you.

MOLLY. I knew it!

NATE. Knew what?

MOLLY. I knew you were hitting on me at that gallery.

NATE. I wasn't hitting on you.

MOLLY. What would you call it?

NATE. I just like being around you.

MOLLY. And here I thought you always hated me.

NATE. Exactly. I want to like, pull your hair.

MOLLY. Nate, stop.

NATE. You get me all riled up.

MOLLY. You're acting like a little kid.

NATE. You're blushing.

MOLLY. I am not.

NATE. You are. You're excited. I excite you.

MOLLY. Oh, come on.

NATE. Let me ask you a question. How often do you and Kev have sex?

MOLLY. NATE!

NATE. I knew it – not that often.

MOLLY. I'll have you know that we have sex twice a week.

NATE. Always? You always do it twice a week? That's depressing.

MOLLY. That is a healthy amount.

NATE. I know – that's why it's depressing. You probably do it twice a week precisely because it's a healthy amount. You guys suck.

MOLLY. Excuse me? Not five minutes ago you wanted what we have and now we suck?

NATE. Yeah.

MOLLY. You're bipolar.

NATE. You are!

MOLLY. I'm getting you an Uber.

(She picks up her phone.)

NATE. Wait – I'm sorry. It's just that you seem like something special and I'm jealous.

MOLLY. (You think I'm special?) Nate...

NATE. And Kevin is so lucky because you're going to take care of him forever.

(Beat.)

Who's going to take care of me?

7. A Bar

(**LIL** *sits at a bar with* **KEVIN**.)

KEVIN. Okay, I'm gonna say something but I don't want you to be mad or offended.

LIL. Okay...but saying that sort of guarantees you're about to say something that will make me mad and offend me.

KEVIN. Your problem, Lil, is that you make Friend Art.

LIL. What's that?

KEVIN. It's art that only your friends come to see, because they have to. So if you want to be successful you need to either make a shitload of friends who feel obligated to support you or start making better art.

LIL. I'm mad and offended.

KEVIN. Yeah, I don't think you are. I think you just feel like you're supposed to say that.

(*Small beat.*)

I saw you setting up today.

LIL. Yeah, you said.

KEVIN. I didn't even know it was you at first. I just saw this little body carrying these heavy lights inside that shitty theater and I thought, who would do that? Even at your age, when she was acting, Molly never would have carried lights.

LIL. What are you trying to say? That for once you actually took me seriously because you were spying on me during tech?

KEVIN. I was impressed. That you, you know, put the work in. So I came to see it. And then, when I was watching your show, I was looking at you and thinking – oh my god. This is terrible. This is so embarrassing and she doesn't care, she's up there going for it and that's amazing.

LIL. Fuck you.

KEVIN. I'm trying to compliment you.

LIL. It doesn't sound that way to me.

KEVIN. I realized that you're the only person I know who still does what they love. And I had this thought. If you're starting off from a place where no one takes you seriously, you kind of have nothing to lose.

LIL. I'm done with this conversation. Thanks for the drink. I hope it was expensive.

KEVIN. I'm talking about myself.

LIL. What?

KEVIN. I'm talking about me. No one takes me seriously. The people at the top of my industry have advanced degrees in Art History. They've worked in galleries and as buyers. They don't get promoted from within.

LIL. So?

KEVIN. So I stayed too long at a job that sounded cool, and paid okay for a guy in his twenties where I could get away with coming in hungover. But now I'm thirty-two and engaged and it's a joke, so what am I supposed to do?

LIL. I don't know. Why are you asking me?

KEVIN. How do you not care what people think of you?

LIL. Are you kidding me? I care insanely what people think of me.

KEVIN. You couldn't. You wouldn't be able to do the things you do if you did.

LIL. I make the art that I make because I feel like I have to, but I want people to like it. And it really hurts me when no one does.

(Small beat.)

KEVIN. Did Molly tell you that we're moving?

LIL. No. Where are you moving? Like Ditmas Park or something?

KEVIN. We're moving to Alexandria, Virginia.

LIL. Shit. Why?

KEVIN. I'm going to law school at GW.

    (Beat.)

I don't want to go to law school at GW.

LIL. So why are you?

KEVIN. Because I feel like I have to. Because I convinced Molly it would be what's best for us. Because I asked her to marry me. Because what the hell else am I going to do? I don't know. There's a lot of reasons.

LIL. Yeah. I guess so.

KEVIN. But I find you very inspiring, Lil. I'd like to help you.

LIL. Help me what?

KEVIN. Help you make something that's not Friend Art.

LIL. I don't know what that means.

KEVIN. Okay, so your show, it's a good start. You look great up there but it needs something more. Like, you know what I was thinking about while I was watching it?

LIL. What?

KEVIN. That Britney VMA performance. You know, the one with the snake, "I'm A Slave 4 U"? Where she was totally at the top of her game and everyone wanted to have sex with her.

LIL. Are you comparing me to Britney Spears right now because that conversation might not be worth the cocktail.

KEVIN. Relax, I'm not comparing you to current Britney, I'm comparing you to 2003 Britney, which is like, a massive compliment.

LIL. Listen Kevin, you may be having some sort of weird life crisis, but I'm a performance artist, okay?

KEVIN. One could argue that Britney shaving her head was one of the best pieces of performance art of the 2000s.

LIL. That was a psychotic break. Not an art piece.

KEVIN. A psychotic break that got a lot of attention.

    (Beat.)

Let me tell you a story. I went to this tiny college.

LIL. Is that the story? Because I already know where you went to school.

KEVIN. No. I went to this tiny college in Vermont – school of lunatics and look at me, you'd never guess it, right? Molly, as you know, went to NYU. And when we first got together we used to go to a lot of shows, music shows. Not people who were famous, just like, people we were friends with. And when we went to shows of the kids I went to school with – the guys are crazy, you can't have a conversation with them afterwards. But the music was great because these guys were freaks, but – they were real musicians. Then, we go to the NYU shows and well – the guys were awesome, we wanted to hang out with them afterwards and do drugs. But the music sucked because these weren't musicians they were just cool guys who wanted to be in a band.

LIL. So what are you saying? That I'm the talented freak or the fun poser?

KEVIN. I think you're both. But right now – you're the wrong combination of both.

LIL. So, you think I'm what – a poser freak?

KEVIN. With the potential to be fun and talented.

LIL. I'm so confused. One minute you're getting me to feel sorry for you, the next you're insulting me.

KEVIN. It's not an insult, Lil. It's the truth. Aren't you always asking us to be honest with you?

LIL. I want you to honestly tell me you like my stuff.

KEVIN. Blind praise won't make you a better artist.

LIL. Neither will blind insults.

KEVIN. Just think about it. What would it look like if you had unlimited resources?

LIL. I don't know. I use the resources I have.

KEVIN. But you should think beyond what you have. You should aim higher.

LIL. But that's a trap. You can aim so high that you never get anything done.

KEVIN. Sure, but you should aim a little higher than the basement.

LIL. Well, I hate pretention, so I don't want to make anything pretentious.

KEVIN. Um, exsquisme – your stuff is so pretentious.

LIL. It's not. Because I don't take myself that seriously.

KEVIN. You take yourself *so* seriously.

LIL. Wrong. I take my art seriously, but I don't take myself seriously while I'm performing it. There's a difference.

KEVIN. I don't think that's coming through the way you want it to then.

LIL. Okay, see – that's a good crit. Comparing me to Britney – wasn't.

KEVIN. I'm holding fast to that being a compliment. But whatever – what else are you trying to say that I might have missed?

LIL. I really just want to say something relatable, you know? Like the thing I do with the snake.

KEVIN. Yes – except a snake puppet is not relatable.

LIL. But it is! Because it's like this self-sabotaging parasite that we all live with.

KEVIN. Why can't it be a man?

LIL. Because it's funnier if it's a snake.

KEVIN. But no one thinks you're trying to be funny.

LIL. Well, in a way, I'm not.

KEVIN. I think everything you're saying should be the reverse – you take the art seriously but not yourself – shouldn't you take yourself seriously but let the art, if it's supposed to be ridiculous anyway, be the thing that's funny?

LIL. But it's not haha funny. It's sad funny.

KEVIN. Yes, but if you let it be haha funny. It wouldn't be Friend Art.

LIL. What would it be?

KEVIN. It would be funny.

LIL. But I'm not a comedian. I'm a performance artist.

KEVIN. Aren't all performing artists in a way performance artists?

LIL. No. They're not.

      (Tiny beat.)

KEVIN. Have you ever met my friend Mikey?

LIL. No. Who is that?

KEVIN. He's a musician. We went to college together.

LIL. One of the freaks you just mentioned?

KEVIN. Yes, but he's a cool freak. Why don't you let me introduce you?

      (Small beat.)

LIL. I have always wanted to use original music. So, if he's cool and good, that might actually be helpful.

KEVIN. Great. There's just one more thing.

LIL. What's that?

KEVIN. Wardrobe.

8. Outside Molly And Kevin's Apartment

(**MOLLY** *is coming home from yoga.* **LIL** *just met with* **KEVIN**.)

MOLLY. Lil.

LIL. Hi!

(**LIL** *tries to hug* **MOLLY**.)

MOLLY. No, don't. I'm so sweaty. Bikram.

LIL. Oh, sorry.

MOLLY. I'm. Sorry do we have plans that I forgot about?

LIL. No?

MOLLY. Um, so, sorry, what are you doing at my apartment?

LIL. Oh, I was just meeting with Kevin.

MOLLY. Sorry?

LIL. He's helping me out.

MOLLY. Helping you out with what, your taxes?

LIL. Is that a joke?

MOLLY. Sort of. Not a funny one I guess.

LIL. Does Kevin do people's taxes?

MOLLY. No – I don't know why I said that. He doesn't even do his own taxes.

LIL. I'm working on a new piece.

MOLLY. That's great. I'm really sorry I missed the last one.

LIL. Don't worry about it.

MOLLY. No, I am. Especially after what happened last time.

LIL. Molly. It's fine.

MOLLY. I should have been there is all I'm trying to say.

LIL. Thanks.

MOLLY. So, sorry, still playing catch-up. Kev is helping you with...what?

LIL. Oh, my new piece.

MOLLY. Really? Like what part?

LIL. I don't know. All of it.

MOLLY. What does that mean?

> *(Joking.)*

He's like producing it.

LIL. Kind of, I don't know. We haven't labeled anything.

MOLLY. Wait, what? Kevin is producing your new piece?

LIL. I mean, I don't know. We're just talking about some stuff.

> *(Small beat.)*

You look surprised.

MOLLY. I just didn't know.

LIL. Oh, well, it's not like a secret – it's just really early – this was just a brainstorm meeting.

MOLLY. Oh, I got it.

LIL. Got what?

MOLLY. Well – it's not like he's really producing it because there's no it yet.

LIL. There's an it.

MOLLY. Okay, so what is it?

LIL. It's my piece.

MOLLY. But you do so much Lil. What is this it? Writing? Directing? Acting? I can never keep track.

LIL. Is that a dig?

MOLLY. No! I want to know.

LIL. Well I told you I'm still figuring it out.

MOLLY. So you don't even know?

LIL. I know.

MOLLY. So why can't you tell me?

LIL. Because I don't want to talk it dry.

MOLLY. Meaning?

LIL. How can I be inspired on the page if I tell the whole thing to you now.

MOLLY. Are you mad at me?

LIL. No, I've just...I've gotta get to work.

MOLLY. On your piece?

LIL. At the restaurant. I'm late.

MOLLY. Sorry. I didn't mean to keep you.

LIL. You didn't. I'm, you know, glad I ran into you.

MOLLY. Me too.

LIL. We should –

MOLLY. Yeah, dinner?

LIL. Or brunch.

MOLLY. Something.

LIL. Definitely.

MOLLY. Soon.

LIL. Yes.

MOLLY. Okay. So, bye Lil.

LIL. Bye Mol.

MOLLY. Bye.

> (**LIL** *walks away.* **MOLLY** *goes inside. They're both confused and kind of mad but not sure why.*)

9. Molly And Kevin's Apartment

(**KEVIN** *is on his iPad.* **MOLLY** *enters.*)

KEVIN. Hey Beautiful.

MOLLY. Hi.

KEVIN. You hungry? I'm gonna order from the noodle place.

MOLLY. I might just drink.

(*She takes a bottle of wine out of the fridge and pours a glass.*)

KEVIN. K, I'm gonna get some of that vegetable udon and some dumplings, we can put it in the fridge if we don't eat it.

MOLLY. Sure.

(*He finishes the order.*)

KEVIN. And...done.

MOLLY. So...I uh, I just saw Lil downstairs. She, um, she mentioned that you guys are working on something together?

KEVIN. Yeah. I'm trying to help her figure some stuff out.

MOLLY. Were you gonna tell me about it?

KEVIN. Of course.

MOLLY. When?

KEVIN. I don't know, probably tonight.

MOLLY. Because it was really embarrassing that she knew something about you that I didn't.

KEVIN. I'm sorry babe, it's not like I was hiding it from you.

MOLLY. You said you were going into work this weekend.

KEVIN. No. I said I'd be working.

MOLLY. Kevin, what's going on here? You don't even like Lil.

(*Small beat.*)

KEVIN. Okay, do you remember last week, I told you that I went to her show when you had that gallery thing?

MOLLY. Yeah. So what? You said it was weird.

KEVIN. It was. It was really weird. But I don't know, for some reason, while I was watching it, and then talking to her afterwards, I felt compelled to try and – I dunno – help her make it better, or something. Like, don't you think it's kind of sad just watching her flail about?

MOLLY. So that's what this is about? You feel sorry for her?

KEVIN. I feel like I can help her.

MOLLY. Look. I think I know what's going on here and I get it, okay? Lil is enigmatic and exciting and she's the kind of person who when you meet her you want to spend all your time with her and figure her out. She's like a drug and she makes you feel cool and good about yourself and it's awesome. At first. But then, you get to know her better and you realize – that she has no clothes.

KEVIN. What?

MOLLY. Like the Emperor. There's nothing there. There's nothing underneath the facade of "Lil." And whatever that thing was you were hoping to become by being friends with her isn't there either. And you start thinking, where did all that time go that I spent supporting her and listening to her and what did I ever really get out of that relationship? I know this, Kev. This happened to me. You saw it. As soon as I stopped thinking she was so amazing, she stopped wanting to be friends with me. So now she's turned her attention to you, and it feels good. I get it. But it's not real.

KEVIN. Man. I thought you'd be happy about this – you're the one who's always saying we should support her.

MOLLY. But that's exactly what I'm talking about. The only reason I was supporting her was because she was my friend and now she's not acting like a very good friend to me.

KEVIN. Okay, but do you think maybe there's a part of you that's a little jealous?

MOLLY. I'm sorry, what?

KEVIN. No, no. I mean, not of her, but of what she does.

MOLLY. What does she do?

KEVIN. Do you ever wish that you were still acting?

MOLLY. No, Kevin. Jesus. Why would you even bring that up?

KEVIN. It's just I remember I was a big part of encouraging you to quit / and –

MOLLY. I quit because I wasn't getting any roles and I didn't want to work in restaurants anymore.

KEVIN. And I said you'd probably be happier with a real job.

MOLLY. Yes. And I am.

KEVIN. But working on this thing with Lil, even just for today, I don't know, it's that it's fun / and I feel stimulated in a way I never have.

MOLLY. It's fun because it isn't your job.

KEVIN. And I started to think about you and feel bad that I played a part in that. I guess all I'm saying is that if you wanted to start auditioning again, I would support you.

MOLLY. Babe, are you on fucking drugs? You can't just start auditioning again at thirty-one when you don't have an agent and your last credit was some shitty unpaid stuff you did when you were twenty-five. That door is closed.

KEVIN. Okay, okay, I / only meant –

MOLLY. I mean maybe if I'd never quit it would be different, I could've gotten better. But now – I mean, come on, what would I do in Virginia – community theatre? Kev. Please. / You're talking like a crazy person.

KEVIN. Let's not talk about Virginia right now.

> *(Beat.)*

I only meant that I don't think you should not do something out of fear.

MOLLY. Oh my god, I am not afraid! I am also not an actor. The fantasy of it was always way better than the reality for me.

KEVIN. But that's what I'm talking about! Isn't the fantasy why you keep going when the reality sucks?

MOLLY. And your creative fantasy is about Lil?

KEVIN. No. I don't know. It's confusing.

MOLLY. Okay, babe. Let's take a step back. What is this really about?

    (Beat.)

KEVIN. I don't wanna just be the old guy.

MOLLY. What?

KEVIN. At GW. The other people in my class. They're gonna be like twenty-four. They'll have graduated and spent two years dicking around before they got their shit together. I spent ten years dicking around. When they're my age they'll be making partner somewhere. I'll be lucky if I'm under thirty-five when I graduate.

MOLLY. See? That makes sense to me.

KEVIN. I need to do something big before I go. Something I can take with me.

MOLLY. And you really think that Lil is that big thing?

KEVIN. Yeah.

MOLLY. Why?

KEVIN. Because she's, I dunno. I think she's kind of brave I guess.

MOLLY. What does that mean?

KEVIN. She listens to me.

MOLLY. She's not a toy, Kev.

KEVIN. I know.

MOLLY. Don't treat her like one.

KEVIN. It's not like that.

MOLLY. Okay. I feel weird about this.

KEVIN. But –

MOLLY. But, if it's something you really want...

KEVIN. Then...

MOLLY. Then...I support you?

KEVIN. Thank you.

    (KEVIN *kisses* **MOLLY.)**

    (The buzzer sounds. He smiles.)

Noodles.

10. Nate's Apartment

(**MOLLY** and **NATE** *lie on opposite ends of*
NATE*'s couch eating ice cream.*)

MOLLY. This is wrong. Ice cream after yoga, we're being bad.

NATE. Naw. We earned it.

MOLLY. Your Om, P.S., is hilarious. It's so loud.

NATE. At least I'm really doing it. Unlike your little apology Om. Like, excuse me for Om-ing.

MOLLY. Whatever.

(*Small beat.*)

I'm glad you weren't busy.

NATE. I'm never really that busy.

MOLLY. What were you doing when I called?

NATE. Dicking around on the guitar.

MOLLY. Why don't you ever record anything new?

NATE. Probably because I don't have the energy to get people to listen to it after.

MOLLY. Nate! I'd love to listen.

NATE. Thanks but that's not what I meant.

(*Beat.*)

(**MOLLY** *looks around.*)

MOLLY. I don't know why you kept talking about our apartment the other day. You have like the nicest apartment I've ever seen.

NATE. Eh, it's good for parties.

MOLLY. What isn't it good for?

NATE. Stuff like this. It's not cozy.

MOLLY. I'm having fun.

(*Beat.*)

NATE. So what are you doing all alone on a Saturday anyway? Where's Kev? Why aren't you guys like on a couple's jog?

MOLLY. Ugh. 'Cause he's with Lil. Working on their weirdo collaboration.

NATE. And you're pissed.

MOLLY. Of course.

NATE. So why don't you say anything about it?

MOLLY. Because then I wouldn't be being supportive.

NATE. But you're not supportive.

MOLLY. Yeah, but he doesn't know that.

NATE. Uh-oh.

MOLLY. What?

NATE. Couples swap?

MOLLY. Shut up.

> *(Tiny beat.)*

Sometimes I think if you and Lil hadn't started dating we wouldn't still be friends.

NATE. You set us up!

MOLLY. I know but it's not like I thought it was actually going to work.

NATE. Thanks.

MOLLY. I just mean that dating you kept her in my life after she left the firm. I wasn't trying to be a bitch.

NATE. Yes you were. But it's okay. You can be a bitch over here. I'm into it.

MOLLY. Come on, seriously, don't you think it's weird for them to just be like, together, alone.

> **(MOLLY** *and* **NATE** *lie on the same couch, head to toe, but still.)*

NATE. And this isn't weird?

MOLLY. No. We've known each other forever. We're like brother and sister.

NATE. I'd go cousins.

MOLLY. Kevin is probably thrilled that we're hanging out.

NATE. But you're not thrilled he's hanging out with Lil.

MOLLY. Because what could he possibly want to help her with?

NATE. Maybe he doesn't want to help her.

MOLLY. What do you mean?

NATE. Maybe he wants to...fuck her?

MOLLY. Excuse me?

NATE. I'm not saying he's trying to. Just maybe he, you know, wants to.

MOLLY. So meeting up with her is what, like, jack-off fuel?

NATE. Yeah, you know, like a fluffer.

MOLLY. Ugh. You're just trying to get a rise out of me. You done?

> *(He hands her his bowl. She takes the bowls into the kitchen, washes them.)*

NATE. I'm just giving you the guy's perspective.

MOLLY. Kevin would never.

NATE. I'm not saying he would.

MOLLY. He would never even think about it.

NATE. How do you know?

MOLLY. Because I know.

NATE. Man.

MOLLY. What?

NATE. He has you trained so fucking well. I've gotta like buy that guy a burger.

MOLLY. Trained?

NATE. Yeah. You never suspect him of anything.

MOLLY. Because he doesn't do anything.

NATE. Burger with fries.

MOLLY. Are you trying to tell me there's something you know about my fiancé that I don't?

NATE. Well, no. Not specifically.

MOLLY. What does that mean?

NATE. It means that I have never seen Kevin step out of line or do anything remotely cheat-like.

MOLLY. So then what are we talking about?

NATE. But non-specifically – all men cheat. They just do. Sorry.

MOLLY. Well, Kevin doesn't.

NATE. That doesn't mean he doesn't want to.

MOLLY. Ugh.

NATE. I'm telling you the truth. I'm treating you like a dude right now. I thought that's what all girls wanted.

MOLLY. Well, I don't want to be treated like a dude.

NATE. What do you want me to treat you like?

MOLLY. Hello? Like a girl.

NATE. If I were treating you like a girl I'd have you out of those yoga pants by now.

MOLLY. Oh, gross Nate. So treating me like a dude is telling me my fiancé is probably cheating on me and treating me like a girl is trying to fuck me? Those cannot be the only two options with you.

NATE. I'm trying to be helpful.

MOLLY. You're not. You're just trying to get me to think that Kevin wants to cheat on me so that I will then cheat on him, with you.

NATE. Dude, you are so full of yourself.

MOLLY. But you just said –

NATE. Yeah, but I was kidding.

MOLLY. Oh my god. I hate you.

NATE. You love me.

MOLLY. That's what you think.

NATE. Hey.

MOLLY. Yeah?

NATE. Thanks for coming over.

MOLLY. Anytime.

11. A Basement Performance Venue

(Music starts and the space is transformed. We are underneath a bar in a basement music venue. It's hot and dirty but cooler than hot and dirty theater spaces.)

(MOLLY and NATE enter. It feels like there are a lot of people here.)

NATE. Huh.

MOLLY. What?

NATE. I used to play here.

MOLLY. Here here?

NATE. Yeah, when I was first starting out.

MOLLY. And now Lil is here. Why?

NATE. I know. I don't know.

MOLLY. Feeling nostalgic?

NATE. Surprisingly, no.

MOLLY. Feeling...?

NATE. Like we are going to need a drink for this. What do you want?

MOLLY. Whatever.

NATE. Be right back.

> *(NATE exits.)*

> *(KEVIN comes up to MOLLY and gives her a hug from behind. He has a happy, excited energy about him.)*

KEVIN. There she is.

MOLLY. Hey babe. How's it going?

KEVIN. Well you know we're nervous but good turn out, right?

MOLLY. Yeah. Who are all these people?

KEVIN. Who knows.

MOLLY. I'm so curious. I can't wait to see it.

KEVIN. Yeah, I mean I don't want to say anything until you do but – well, just wait.

MOLLY. I'm excited.

KEVIN. Did you come by yourself?

MOLLY. Nate picked me up.

KEVIN. You guys have been hanging out a lot lately.

MOLLY. Not as much as you and Lil.

*(**NATE** returns with the drinks.)*

NATE. Hey man.

KEVIN. Nate. Buddy.

(They hug.)

Thanks so much for coming.

NATE. Yeah – I'm, you know, real curious what you two have been up to.

KEVIN. And thanks for keeping an eye on Molly while I've been so busy.

NATE. Aw –

*(**NATE** puts his hand on **MOLLY**'s shoulder.)*

She's been keeping an eye on me.

KEVIN. Okay, well. Right. See you after.

*(**KEVIN** exits.)*

NATE. You okay?

MOLLY. Yeah.

NATE. You sure?

MOLLY. I'm just curious.

NATE. Me too.

MOLLY. Thanks for the drink.

(Lights go down.)

(Blackout.)

*(We hear **LIL**'s voice all around us:)*

LIL. Did you ever imagine that an animal was in bed with you? A spider? A mouse? A rat? A SNAKE?

(Start music.)

*(*LIL* kicks a door open and we see that she is wearing a full-body, skin-tight snake costume.)*

(She approaches a mic and starts to sing.)

THE SNAKE. THE SNAKE. THE SNAKE.
HE'S IN MY BEEEEED. HE'S IN MY BEEEEED.
HE'S IN MY BEEEEED. HE'S IN MY BEEEEED.

*(*LIL* owns the stage. She's not afraid to get down on the ground, get dirty. She has the audience in the palm of her hand.)*

HE'S IN MY... HE'S IN MY... HE'S IN MY...THE SNAKE.
HE'S IN MY... HE'S IN MY... HE'S IN MY...THE SNAKE.

HE GRABBED MY TOOOEEEE. HE'S IN MY BEEEEED.
HE GRABBED MY TOOOEEEE. HE'S IN MY HEEEAAADDD.

*(*LIL* gets into a full-body war with herself and with the snake. Eventually she is able to break free of him and to slide out of her skin. To shed the snake.)*

THE SNAKE. MY TOE. MY BED.
HE'S IN. MY BED. THE SNAKE.
MY TOE. MY SNAKE. MY BED.

HE'S IN MY BEEEEDDDD.

(The costume is now another being. There's LIL. *And there's the snake. He no longer has control over her. She grabs him by the neck.)*

*(*LIL* fucks the snake. She owns it. When she's finished with him, he's limp – weak. Dead, maybe. She killed him.)*

(She addresses the audience.)

He's soft now and I can rest.
If I let him stay and hold him,
will he love me more or less?
It's going to be so awkward

when we see each other,
Tomorrow,
on the internet!

> *(She screams in triumph.)*
> *(Blackout.)*

12. Nate's Apartment

(**NATE** and **MOLLY** go to **NATE**'s loft. He hands her a drink.)

NATE. Did you talk to Kev?

MOLLY. Ya. I texted and told him we were getting something to eat 'cause neither of us ate dinner. I just had to get out of there you know?

NATE. Sure.

MOLLY. God that was fucking weird. Like, seriously Nate, Kevin has been talking about this project as the thing that's going to, I dunno, change his life or something and it's Lil fucking a snake in fishnet stockings?? Are you kidding me? Am I supposed to be like, "Congrats"?

NATE. Uh, yeah. I dunno.

MOLLY. I mean, is that how you think Kevin sees Lil?

NATE. Loaded question. Not answering.

MOLLY. Come on, don't you think it's weird?

NATE. The crowd was into it.

MOLLY. Sure, but think of all of the other shows of hers we've seen. They're undergrad theatrics, they're nonsense. This was like Pussy Riot meets Ke$ha.

NATE. Which is awesome.

MOLLY. But doesn't it make you angry. That she's up there pretending to be a musician. When that's what you are?

NATE. It doesn't make me angry if it's real.

MOLLY. But how could it be real?

(**NATE** takes out a bag of coke and starts to cut it on a tray on his coffee table.)

NATE. This doesn't weird you out does it?

MOLLY. Um, no, no, 'course not.

NATE. Do you want some?

MOLLY. (She hesitates, and then:) Yeah. Sure.

(They both do lines.)

MOLLY. Everyone is freaked out before they get married, right?

NATE. I don't know, dude. You're asking the wrong guy.

MOLLY. Is it weird that the time we've been engaged has been the most distant we've ever been in our relationship? Or do you naturally have to grow apart a little to be able to see the relationship clearly and decide you actually want to be together? I mean, Kevin must be freaking out, right? What was tonight if not a freak out?

NATE. Are you freaking out?

MOLLY. I didn't think so, but I'm here, in your loft doing drugs with you, and I don't do drugs. And I told Kevin not to do drugs anymore either.

NATE. I'm sorry. I shouldn't have –

(He tries to maybe put the drugs away.)

MOLLY. No. It's good. I want to have fun tonight. I want to have a big night!

NATE. Just take it easy, killer. I'm gonna put some music on.

*(While his back is turned, **MOLLY** cuts another line and takes it. **NATE** puts a record on. Music begins to play. He comes back.)*

MOLLY. Do you ever feel like you were born in the wrong decade?

NATE. Eh, sometimes I wish "Climbing Up My Throat" had come out a few years earlier, like if I could have been solidly in that nineties scene instead of on the tail end of it.

MOLLY. That's not what I mean. I mean like, sometimes I think I was born in the wrong decade. If I could've just been born like – fifteen to twenty years earlier. It's not like I want to be young in the sixties or anything but maybe like, the eighties? I think I would've been a really amazing yuppie. Work in an office in Manhattan. Eat like shrimp scampi, wear Laura Ashley. No one in the eighties was trying to be cool. Everyone was just trying to be rich. And now it's like everyone needs to be cool, but they also still want to be rich, but the rich part has to be like a secret. If it were the eighties I could just work at a fancy law firm and everyone would be like cool. No one would ever give me that look like, "Aw, you didn't have a better idea." I don't want to feel like I should quit my job to make like, artisinal Etsy bullshit that you can really only do if you have a rich dad anyway. Don't you hate how everyone calls their hobbies their jobs now? Like, in the eighties you'd be like, "Oh, that girl is really into crafts," and now you have to be like, "Oh, she's a ceramicist."

NATE. I dated a ceramicist once.

MOLLY. Of course you did. And, seriously, what is the point of buying one-of-a-kind ceramics when everyone's bowls still look the same?

NATE. Yeah, dude. I dunno.

MOLLY. Do you wanna know what else I hate? Yoga.

NATE. No! You're my yoga buddy.

MOLLY. I know. But I hate it. I just feel like I'm supposed to go. Like, you know that thing, that out-of-body thing, that people say they feel in yoga?

NATE. Yeah. I love that thing.

MOLLY. I've never felt it. I have no idea what the hell anybody is talking about.

(*She tries to cut another line.*)

NATE. Maybe just cool it for a sec? You don't have to take one like every five seconds.

MOLLY. Whatever, I know, I mean I didn't realize it had only been like five seconds.

(**NATE** *moves the tray with drugs off the coffee table.*)

You don't need to like hide the drugs from me, I'm not the one who has a problem with drugs, remember?

NATE. I'm just...cleaning up.

MOLLY. And I don't want to move to Virginia.

NATE. Who's moving to Virgina?

MOLLY. Me and Kevin. Before the wedding.

NATE. Wait. Are you joking?

MOLLY. Oh. I thought you knew.

NATE. No man, I didn't fucking know that. Shit, why does everyone always leave?

MOLLY. I dunno. But I wish there was a way I didn't have to. Do you know where I really want to move?

NATE. Where?

(She looks around his apartment.)

MOLLY. Back to Manhattan. But I want everyone else to move back with me. But I only want to do it if I'm rich. And I want to be rich. Is that like so horrible to say?

NATE. Eh, I mean, it depends who you're saying it around.

MOLLY. The eighties were just like my time, you know, and I missed them.

NATE. Well we're doing coke so that's pretty eighties.

MOLLY. Can I smoke in here?

KEVIN. Sure.

MOLLY. Do you have any cigs?

(He gives her one. She lights it. He gets an ashtray and puts it in front of her.)

God. I fucking love smoking.

NATE. I do too.

MOLLY. You know what else I love?

NATE. Huh?

MOLLY. McDonald's. I'm so pissed people made all those documentaries about how it's made and now we can't eat it anymore.

NATE. You can still eat it.

MOLLY. I know, but it's wrong. Wanna hear a secret?

NATE. Sure.

MOLLY. Sometimes if I'm craving McDonald's I'll bring a brown paper bag from home and make them put it in that instead of one of theirs.

NATE. Everything in your refrigerator is organic and you're walking around with secret McNuggets, that's hilarious.

MOLLY. Where's the coke?

NATE. I think you're good, dude. Just, chill.

I can't believe Kev didn't tell me you guys are moving.

MOLLY. Maybe he doesn't want to think about it.

(Beat.)

Can I take, just like, one more line. I'm fine, I promise.

NATE. Okay.

(She goes to the mantle and does another line.)

MOLLY. You want?

(She hands him the bill. He goes to the mantle as well. Does another one.)

Do you wanna hear something selfish?

NATE. Sure.

MOLLY. I wanted it to be bad tonight.

NATE. Why?

MOLLY. Because I'm supposed to be the creative one in our relationship. Not him.

NATE. You work at a law firm.

MOLLY. But I wanted to be an actress.

NATE. When?

MOLLY. Nate, you came to my plays!

NATE. Oh right. The ones with the...

MOLLY. Just stop. God. It's embarrassing. Wanting to act past high school is just so fucking embarrassing.

(She puts her head in her hands.)

NATE. Hey. I'm sorry I didn't remember.

MOLLY. Wanna hear something funny? Molly Hart is the kind of actress who makes you believe that the best time in her life was senior year of high school. She seems better suited to Sweet Valley High than Shakespeare. It's a shame she's already too old for her own show on the Disney Channel.

NATE. What's that?

MOLLY. My review.

NATE. From what?

MOLLY. Fringe Fest *Midsummer*. It was a slow week so we got the *Times* to come. Everyone I know read that.

NATE. You quit acting because you got a bad review for amateur Shakespeare? Molly. Come on, who gives a shit?

MOLLY. And you know what? I did have fun senior year of high school, do I have to apologize for that for the rest of my life?

    (**NATE** *laughs.*)

It's not funny.

NATE. It is funny.

MOLLY. Fine, it's funny. I was never that good. I was supposed to get weeded out. And I'm fine with that except –

NATE. Except what?

MOLLY. Except there are these girls I used to see at auditions all the time, and they weren't any better than me. And I used to feel so superior to them after I quit, because I had a real job and health insurance and could go out to dinner. But now, occasionally, I'll see one of them on a commercial or a TV show or something. And I see them post stuff on Facebook and I don't think they do still work in restaurants, I think they're doing it, you know, like they're really doing it and I wonder if maybe, that could've been me too.

NATE. You can still do whatever you want, Molly.

MOLLY. No I can't. I got weeded out like I was supposed to.

NATE. So did I, in a way.

MOLLY. No you didn't. You're really good. And you're famous.

NATE. Not really. Not anymore.

MOLLY. I'd still take your story over mine.

NATE. It has its own set of downfalls.

MOLLY. Like what?

NATE. Like, I have enough money to do nothing. And I'm just famous enough that I can't get a real job so I spend most of my time going nuts and doing drugs.

MOLLY. Rich person problems.

NATE. It's an empty life, Molly. One that could end in me dying. For realz.

MOLLY. We won't let that happen.

NATE. You're moving to Virginia.

(Beat.)

MOLLY. Nate.

NATE. Yeah?

MOLLY. You think I'm pretty, right?

NATE. Of course.

MOLLY. And you would have sex with me?

NATE. Hypothetically.

MOLLY. And that's why you've been flirting with me so much. Because you think that I'm someone who's like, hot, and not because you're just fucking with me?

NATE. Well, yeah, I think you're hot. But also I'm, you know, fucking with you.

MOLLY. But if things didn't work out with Kevin, you think there'd be guys who'd like me?

NATE. Of course.

MOLLY. You'd like me?

NATE. I already like you, Mol. You know that.

MOLLY. That makes me feel better.

NATE. Hey, it's okay. Come here.

(He hugs her. Holds her.)

MOLLY. I don't want you to think I don't like my life. Or that I don't love Kevin.

NATE. I know. I don't think that.

MOLLY. But, you know, sometimes things change and that's okay too.

NATE. What?

(*She tries to kiss him.*)

WHOA. What are you doing?

(*Backing away from her.*)

MOLLY. What do you mean?

NATE. What do you think is going on here?

MOLLY. Um, you know, we've been spending all this time together. I thought –

NATE. You thought what? That I was going to sleep with my best friend's fiancée? What kind of guy do you think I am?

MOLLY. You've been flirting with me like crazy.

NATE. That's just flirting. It's fun because I know you'll never do it.

(**MOLLY** *gets quiet, sad.*)

MOLLY. It's so unfair being a girl. You get to say whatever you want to me. And I can either be cool which means you say whatever you want and I smile and laugh it off. Or I can be lame which means you say whatever you want and I get offended – but that's it – all I get are facial expressions. You can say whatever you want to me and Kevin can do whatever he wants to Lil – but when it's all over, me and Lil don't matter.

NATE. I think I should take you home. I shouldn't have done drugs with you. I'm sorry.

MOLLY. I thought you liked me.

NATE. I do like you.

MOLLY. I thought – never mind. It's too fucking embarrassing.

(*She puts her jacket on.*)

NATE. Where are you going?

MOLLY. I'm going out.

NATE. I don't think that's a good idea. I'm gonna take you home, okay?

MOLLY. Fuck you, Nate. You're not my boyfriend, you're not my husband, you're not my father, you're not even really my friend. I'm going out.

(**MOLLY** *exits.*)

13. Molly And Kevin's Apartment

> (**LIL** *and* **KEVIN** *drink champagne and dance.*
> **LIL** *is iPod djing.* **MOLLY** *enters. She's been
> out by herself looking for the "fun" and not
> finding it. She's still coked-up but starting to
> come down.*)

MOLLY. What are you guys doing?

LIL. I'm DJing.

KEVIN. DJ Lil!

> (**KEVIN** *dances over to* **MOLLY**, *kisses her.*)

You're home late my love.

> (**KEVIN** *and* **LIL** *keep dancing throughout the
> following.* **MOLLY** *stands to the side, watching
> them.*)

How's your BFF Nate?

MOLLY. He's good.

KEVIN. What were you guys doing out so late?

MOLLY. Nothing really, it just seemed like you guys were talking to a bunch of people after the show and we didn't want to get in the way.

KEVIN. That's fine but you didn't have to leave.

LIL. Did you get to meet Mikey at least?

MOLLY. That was Mikey? From college?

LIL. He wrote all the music. I am obsessed with him.

KEVIN. Babe. Did you see how many people were there?

MOLLY. Yeah. Who were all those people?

LIL. People who love meeee! And Mikey.

MOLLY. You guys are drunk.

LIL. We're celebrating! Your Kev is a genius, putting my monologues to music was totally brillz!

KEVIN. Hell ya it was!

MOLLY. But no one could hear them.

LIL. Yes, they could.

MOLLY. And the one they could hear they were laughing at.

KEVIN. They're supposed to laugh. It's funny.

MOLLY. But, Lil – you didn't write those monologues to be funny. Those are sincere.

LIL. It's just kind of different now.

MOLLY. *(To* **KEVIN.***)* Why does she have to be naked?

LIL. I wasn't naked.

MOLLY. Lil, I'm sorry. I'm not trying to judge. But that just...that just didn't seem like you up there.

    *(***LIL** *turns off the music.)*

LIL. Oh my god. I can't believe you're doing this again.

MOLLY. What am I doing?

LIL. I finally made something that it seems like people might get something out of and you're trying to shit all over it. This time your genius note is that it didn't seem like me? I finally have a hit and it can't be me? What, you think something can only be mine if it's a failure?

MOLLY. You're spinning what I'm saying.

LIL. I mean, Jesus, I have tried so hard to ignore your passive-aggressive comments about my work.
I don't know if it's jealousy or / what but –

MOLLY. Wait – you think I'm jealous of you? That's insane.

LIL. Right. Because I'm such a fuck-up that no one could ever be jealous of me?

KEVIN. Okay, girls. I feel like emotions are probably running a little high right now and everyone is saying things they don't mean. Lil, I think Molly was just giving her opinion on what we did tonight.

LIL. / What *I* did tonight.

MOLLY. Please don't speak for me, Kevin. I'm not jealous of you, Lil. I'm not jealous you were singing some shitty songs that make fun of things you wrote because they meant something to you and I'm not jealous that everyone in there was either laughing at you or imagining fucking you. And I have been a good friend to you, you are the one who stopped returning my calls so you could run around with my fiancé behind my back. So if you wanna feel good about yourself by pretending to be a victim and make me the villain in all of this go right ahead but please at least take a second to understand it's a lie – and then, by all means live it.

(NATE enters, sees MOLLY.)

NATE. Jesus. You scared the shit out of me.

KEVIN. / Hey?

MOLLY. I'm fine, clearly.

KEVIN. Why wouldn't she be fine?

NATE. She did a shitload of coke / and then ran out of my house into the middle of the street and almost got run over by a fucking cab before like, disappearing all together. I looked all over the goddamn city for you.

KEVIN. She did what?

LIL. You never chased after me.

NATE. That's different, you were always storming out. Molly's not –

MOLLY. Not what? You think I'm less capable of looking after myself, than Lil?

LIL. What's that supposed to mean?

KEVIN. What were you guys even doing?

MOLLY. We were celebrating your show babe.

KEVIN. Without us, and doing, "a shitload" of coke? Nate, can I talk to you for a sec.

MOLLY. No! The men do not need to go off and talk, without the women. I am fine. I am home. You guys were in our apartment together, we were in Nate's apartment together, big fucking deal, everyone needs to apologize and no one needs to apologize. It's fine. Let's just forget it and like, start fucking packing.

(MOLLY starts to cry. KEVIN goes over to her.)

KEVIN. I think you guys should leave.

NATE. I'm really sorry, man.

KEVIN. We'll talk later.

LIL. Thanks for everything you did to help with the show, Kevin.

>(**NATE** *and* **LIL** *exit.*)
>
>(*Silence.*)

MOLLY. I'm actually starting to look forward to moving to Virginia.

KEVIN. Oh, babe.

>(**KEVIN** *goes to* **MOLLY.**)

I'm sorry I yelled at you. I think we all just got a little wrapped up in the moment. Those guys are crazy, you know that. He shouldn't have taken advantage of you like that?

MOLLY. What?

KEVIN. Well, you know, hanging out with Nate can be a little peer pressure-y. I shouldn't have gotten mad at you.

MOLLY. No one peer pressured me, Kevin. I'm not a teenager.

KEVIN. I'm letting you off the hook.

MOLLY. I don't want to be let off the hook. I wanna talk about what's happening that's making us both act like this. I can't marry you with all these secrets.

KEVIN. Fine. Let's talk.

MOLLY. Okay.

KEVIN. Molly, I love you so much.

MOLLY. I know. I love you too.

KEVIN. But –

MOLLY. But?

KEVIN. I don't know if I can move to Virginia.

MOLLY. What?

KEVIN. Okay before we start talking about this, remember that you didn't want to move there in the first place.

MOLLY. Kev. You paid the deposit on your tuition. Your parents are ready to help us put a down payment on a house. Our wedding is less than three months away!

KEVIN. I know, I'm not confused about that. I know I want to marry you. I'm just – not sure I want to go to law school anymore.

MOLLY. Why?

KEVIN. ...Did you see how many people were there tonight?

MOLLY. Oh god. Please tell me you're joking.

KEVIN. Look. Law school was always the plan if I never figured out something I wanted to do more, but now, I feel like, just under the gun, I figured it out.

MOLLY. Kevin, no. You can't just go switching teams on me.

KEVIN. What?

MOLLY. We're supposed to be the people rolling their eyes at this kind of thing. But I don't want to have to roll my eyes at you. Because I love you.

KEVIN. Are you telling me you were rolling your eyes tonight? You didn't like it.

MOLLY. I liked it.

KEVIN. Tell me the truth.

MOLLY. I liked it, Kev. What do you want me to say? Why do you care so much?

KEVIN. Because I did that. It's important to me.

MOLLY. What exactly did you do though? I don't understand.

KEVIN. All of it! I thought of it! It was my idea and it's important to me that you respect it.

MOLLY. I can't believe we're having this conversation. I can't believe it's you asking me to tell you what I think.

KEVIN. I can't believe you won't.

  (Beat.)

MOLLY. It's been a weird night.

KEVIN. Yeah.

MOLLY. What now?

KEVIN. Dunno. Bed? Sleep it off. Talk more tomorrow? I really love you, Molly.

MOLLY. I know. I love you too. You go in. I'm gonna stay out here for awhile.

KEVIN. K.

> *(He kisses her cheek and walks into their bedroom.)*

14. A Restaurant

(**MOLLY** *walks into the restaurant where* **LIL**
works.)

MOLLY. Hi.

LIL. Hey.

(*Tiny beat.*)

Do you need a table?

MOLLY. No. I just wanted to talk to you.

LIL. Well, I'm working so...

MOLLY. Five minutes.

LIL. K.

(*They walk to the side.*)

MOLLY. So...how are you?

LIL. What do you mean?

MOLLY. You know, like, after your show. How do you feel?

LIL. I feel fucking great.

MOLLY. Oh, that's good.

LIL. I'm doing another one this weekend.

MOLLY. You are? Kev didn't mention anything about –

LIL. Mikey set it up. His friend's band needs an opener.

MOLLY. Oh – does Kev know?

LIL. I think we told him, but you know, the show is kinda
    just rolling now. Kevin doesn't need to be there for
    every performance. It's really my and Mikey's thing.

MOLLY. But I mean, it's kinda like Kev's thing too.

LIL. You know what Kevin actually did on the show, right?

MOLLY. Yeah, he produced it.

LIL. He introduced me to Mikey.

MOLLY. And...?

LIL. And he came to our rehearsals and was like our biggest
    cheerleader, always tweeting about the show and taking

Snapchat videos. And he bought us lunch a few times which was really cool of him –

MOLLY. So what are you saying? That's all he did, bought lunch and tweeted?

LIL. I'm saying that Mikey made all the music. I wrote all the lyrics. I choreographed it. Mikey found the venue and I made the snake.

MOLLY. So Kevin didn't do anything?

(Small beat.)

Kevin is the idiot.

LIL. You mean instead of the idiot being me?

MOLLY. That's not what I said.

LIL. But it's what you meant, right?

MOLLY. No. I thought –

LIL. I know what you thought. And it's why I was so angry last night when you kept telling me that I hadn't made this. Like I'd been manipulated in some way, that it wasn't me.

(Small beat.)

Everything I make is mine, Molly. Period. That's who I am.

MOLLY. So I guess I'm the idiot. Kevin and I are both the idiots.

LIL. Shouldn't you be happy? I mean you obviously didn't like him working with me.

MOLLY. You're right. I didn't. But that doesn't mean I don't feel bad for him now that you're pushing him out.

LIL. I'm not pushing him out! He didn't make a place for himself.

MOLLY. Or maybe you didn't leave one open for him –

LIL. Molly! That doesn't even make sense. And I know you don't really want Kevin to keep working with me. So why are you really here?

MOLLY. …I don't know.

(*Beat.*)

MOLLY. God, Lil. I have so many conflicting opinions about what you did.

LIL. That's great, though! That means you're thinking about it.

MOLLY. So that's all you care about? My opinion. Not me. Not our friendship. Just what I think of you?

LIL. Do I want you to take me seriously and not think I'm a joke? Of course! You turned on me first, Molly.

MOLLY. Well, we turned on each other, I guess.

LIL. No. I never turned on you.

MOLLY. You did. I don't know the order. But you did.

(*Beat.*)

I felt really protective of you during your show. I'm sorry if you find that offensive, but it's true.

LIL. It's okay. It's not offensive if it's coming from a good place.

MOLLY. It really was! But then, that was all wrapped up in being angry at Kevin and not understanding why he wanted this so badly. And also not wanting him to fail and really wanting him to fail at the same time.

LIL. And wanting me to fail.

MOLLY. And wanting you to succeed too. And.

(*Beat.*)

And being jealous. Because that kind of thing isn't a part of my life anymore.

LIL. I'm sorry.

MOLLY. You don't have to apologize for that.

(*Beat.*)

LIL. When do you guys move?

MOLLY. A couple of months.

LIL. That'll fly.

MOLLY. I know it will.

(Beat.)

And of course, it'd be nice to see you before we go. Really see you I mean.

LIL. We can make that happen. But now, I should probably get back to work.

MOLLY. Sure.

*(**MOLLY** starts to go.)*

LIL. Hey Mol –

MOLLY. Yeah.

LIL. It's just nerves. Everybody has 'em before they get married.

MOLLY. Right.

LIL. Kev's smart. He'll be a good lawyer.

MOLLY. Mmm.

*(**MOLLY** exits.)*

15. Nate's Apartment

(**LIL**, *looking way more "punk rock," comes to* **NATE***'s loft. She has an "undercut" of some kind.*)

LIL. Hi.

NATE. Hey. I put all your stuff in that closet next to the bathroom.

LIL. Thanks.

(**LIL** *goes into the other room.*)

NATE. You look different.

LIL. No I don't.

NATE. You do. You look like you're trying to dress how you think someone in a band about to go on tour should dress.

(**LIL** *comes back out with a large trash bag.*)

LIL. Listen, I just came to pick up this stuff, okay?

(*She starts to sort through her stuff in the bag. She stops, upset.*)

Why would you say that to me?

NATE. I was just making an observation.

LIL. No you weren't. You're making fun of me.

NATE. If you're actually doing this you shouldn't care what people think.

LIL. Why are you being so mean to me?

NATE. I'm giving you advice.

LIL. You're trying to get in my head before I leave.

NATE. Do you know how long I studied music?

LIL. Your whole life, I know.

NATE. I started playing guitar when I was five.

LIL. I'm not pretending to be a musician. I'm a performer. Mikey's the musician. I know that.

NATE. I'm just saying you should rethink your outfit.

LIL. Thanks.

(Beat.)

NATE. When do you leave?

LIL. Next week.

NATE. You know it's not glamorous at this level, right? You'll be sleeping on the floor most of the time.

LIL. I know.

NATE. And no one is going to clean up after you.

LIL. I know.

NATE. And you can't run home to your parents when you don't like your accommodations.

LIL. Just stop, please. I just came to get my stuff.

NATE. I'm trying to prepare you for what it's like. No one out there is obligated to like you. No one coming is going to know you personally.

LIL. I'm looking forward to that.

NATE. I'm not trying to get in your head.

LIL. Okay.

NATE. But I don't want you to leave thinking what you did was okay, either.

LIL. What did I do?

NATE. Do you have any idea who Kevin is?

LIL. A guy in law school? Molly's husband?

NATE. He is the greatest guy ever. He's one of the only people I really trust. And you fucked him.

LIL. No I didn't.

NATE. You used him.

LIL. How could I have used him when he was trying to use me?

NATE. He was trying to help you. Would you be doing what you're doing right now if it wasn't for him?

LIL. No. But that doesn't mean I owe him anything.

NATE. Want to know one of the reasons Kevin is so great?

LIL. Hm?

NATE. Sometimes when we go out – he pays.

LIL. So?

NATE. I try to and he's like, "No buddy, I got this." And he pays. He won't let me.

LIL. I feel like you're trying to say something about me right now. Like what, you're pissed we never went Dutch?

NATE. No, Lil, I liked treating you, you know that. But you never even offered.

LIL. Because you have so much money and I'm so broke. And you know, we were dating and I'm a girl.

NATE. You can't have it both ways. You can't say you're a feminist and expect me to always pay for you.

LIL. Do you want me to like, write you a check right now? Is that what you're saying?

(She takes out her wallet.)

I have like twenty dollars. Here – take it.

NATE. God, no. Gross. Put your wallet away. What are you doing?

*(**LIL** puts her wallet away.)*

LIL. Anyway it's not even true. When we went out with those guys, you always paid for everyone. Always.

NATE. Get off the money thing, Lil. It's not about the money!

It's that he considers other people. How they might feel. That's all I was trying to say.

LIL. You think I'm not considering how Kevin feels about what I'm doing? It's not my job to give other people a purpose in life. You have to do that for yourself.

NATE. I think he was trying to.

LIL. Trying like I was? Trying like you were when you started? I don't think so. They're ordinary, Nate.

NATE. And you're very young. It's useful to remember that you don't know everything yet.

LIL. That's your great piece of wisdom for me?

NATE. Everyone is ordinary, Lil. Even you. You're ordinary too.

LIL. What would you tell someone trying to give you this kind of lecture when you were my age.

NATE. Probably to eat a dick.

LIL. Exactly.

NATE. I just want you to admit that he helped you.

LIL. Fine. He helped me. But that doesn't mean he made me. And I'm not giving him credit for that.

NATE. Look. I'm not saying it's his and not yours.

LIL. Aren't you?

NATE. No.

LIL. Okay. Thanks for keeping this stuff for me.

(She picks up her bag.)

NATE. You're gonna leave like that?

LIL. I don't know what else to say.

NATE. Don't cut and run, Lil. It's a good way to ensure you don't have any friends when you get back.

LIL. You don't want to be my friend, Nate.

NATE. If I didn't want to be your friend, I wouldn't be having this conversation with you.

LIL. What you want, is to be this big man now and have this talk with me about your good friend Kevin. I bet you guys had like weepy beers about law school before they left and you probably threw him a bachelor party and got him a stripper or something and you thought you were doing all of that because you're his friend but actually you just feel guilty that you were messing around with his wife. And that's what this conversation is about too.

NATE. Nothing happened between me and Molly.

LIL. You use people too, it happens.

NATE. You don't know what you're talking about.

LIL. Actually I do. Because like I keep trying to tell all of you, and none of you want to believe it, I'm not a fucking idiot.

NATE. I'm not that guy, Lil.

LIL. We are who we are.

NATE. You know, I wanted to wish you good luck, but now I kind of hate you.

>*(She smiles.)*

LIL. Yeah, so what else is new?

>*(Small beat.)*

Any more parting advice before I go?

NATE. Yeah. Don't fuck your bandmates.

LIL. The snake and I keep it very professional.

>*(Small beat.)*

And I don't really think you're a bad guy.

>*(Smiling.)*

Even if you hate me.

NATE. Oh, Lil.

>*(He sighs.)*

Come here.

>*(He gives her a hug.)*

I'll be rooting for you, okay?

LIL. You will?

NATE. Sure

>*(Beat)*

I just wish you hadn't gotten this stupid haircut.

>*(She looks up at him.)*

LIL. It'll grow.

>*(She heads out. He watches her go.)*
>*(Blackout.)*

End of Play